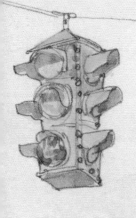

Some ecial

In memory of Frances Oldham, my grandmother
—P. C. M.

For my brother, Billy
—J. P.

ISBN 0-439-45624-X

Text copyright © 2001 by Patricia C. McKissack.
Illustrations copyright © 2001 by Jerry Pinkney. All rights reserved.
Published by Scholastic Inc., 557 Broadway, New York, NY 10012,
by arrangement with Atheneum Books for Young Readers,
Simon & Schuster Children's Publishing Division. SCHOLASTIC
and associated logos are trademarks and/or
registered trademarks of Scholastic Inc.

12 11 10 9 8 7 6 5 4 3 2 1   2 3 4 5 6 7/0

Printed in the U.S.A.   08

First Scholastic printing, September 2002

Book design by Ann Bobco

The text of this book is set in Garamond BE.
The illustrations are rendered in pencil and watercolor on paper.

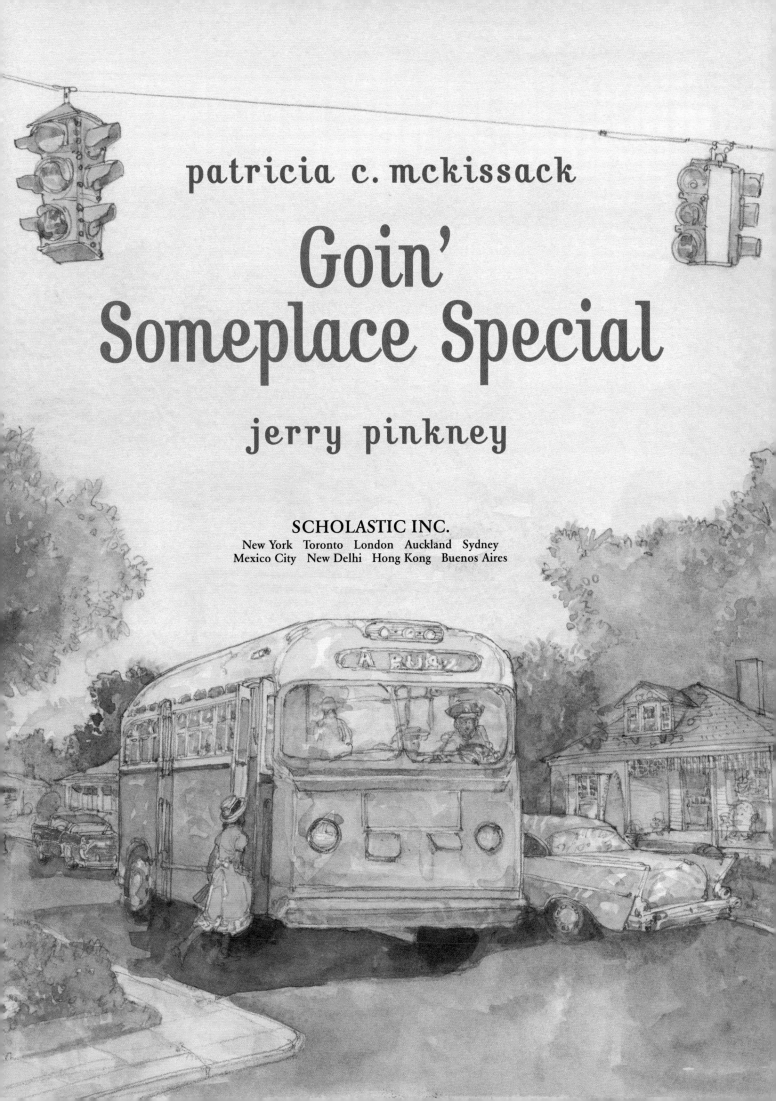

patricia c. mckissack

Goin' Someplace Special

jerry pinkney

SCHOLASTIC INC.
New York Toronto London Auckland Sydney
Mexico City New Delhi Hong Kong Buenos Aires

'Tricia Ann was about to burst with excitement. Crossing her fingers and closing her eyes, she blurted out her question. "Mama Frances, may I go to Someplace Special by myself, today? Pretty please? I know where to get off the bus and what streets to take and all."

Although it had another name, 'Tricia Ann always called it Someplace Special because it was her favorite spot in the world.

"Please may I go? Pretty please with marshmallows on top?"

"I don't know if I'm ready to turn you loose in the world," Mama Frances answered, tying the sash of 'Tricia Ann's dress. "Goin' off alone is a mighty big step."

"I'm ready," the girl said, taking a giant leap across the floor. "See what a big step I can make?"

Mama Frances chuckled, all the time studying her granddaughter's face. "I trust you'll be particular, and remember everything I've told you."

"I will, I will," 'Tricia Ann said, real confident-like. Suddenly, her smile grew into a full grin. "So you're saying I can go?"

"I reckon . . . But you best hurry on 'fore I change my mind."

Pulling her pocketbook up on her shoulder, 'Tricia Ann blew her grandmother a thank-you kiss. Then she rushed out the door and down the sidewalk.

"And no matter what," Mama Frances called after her, "hold yo' head up and act like you b'long to somebody."

At the corner a green and white bus came to a jerky stop and hissed. When the doors folded back, 'Tricia Ann bounded up the steps and dropped in the fare same as when Mama Frances was with her.

The girl squared her shoulders, walked to the back, and took a seat behind the Jim Crow sign that said: COLORED SECTION.

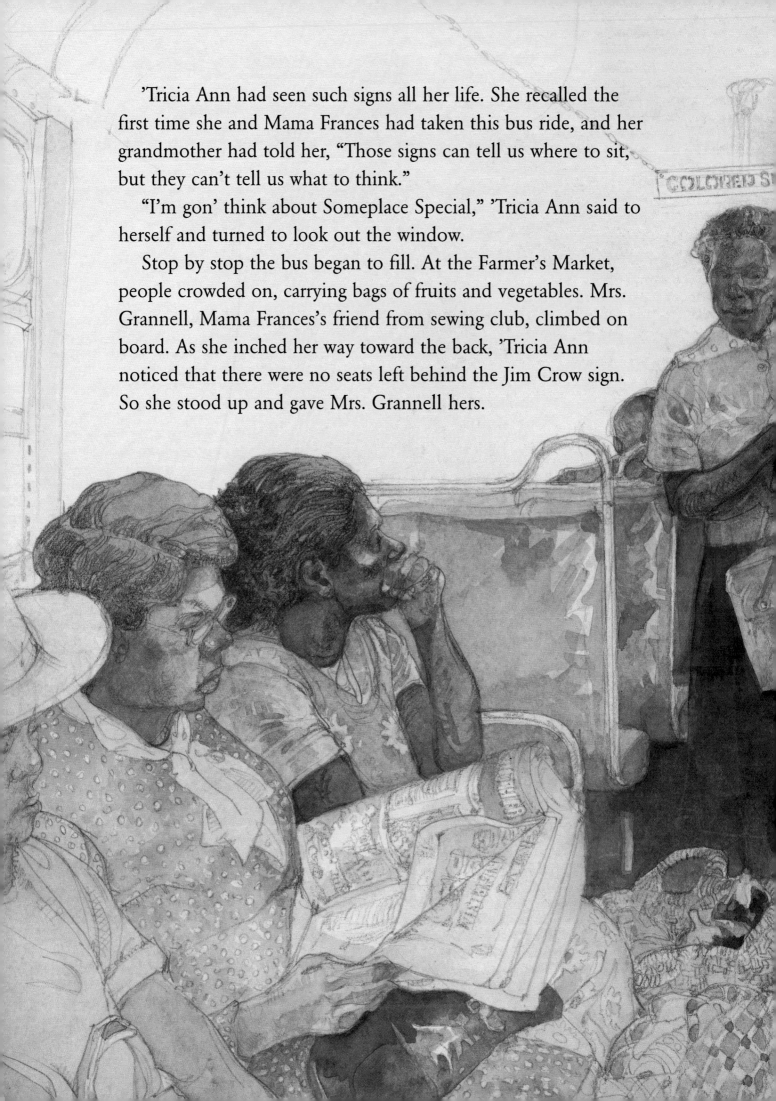

'Tricia Ann had seen such signs all her life. She recalled the first time she and Mama Frances had taken this bus ride, and her grandmother had told her, "Those signs can tell us where to sit, but they can't tell us what to think."

"I'm gon' think about Someplace Special," 'Tricia Ann said to herself and turned to look out the window.

Stop by stop the bus began to fill. At the Farmer's Market, people crowded on, carrying bags of fruits and vegetables. Mrs. Grannell, Mama Frances's friend from sewing club, climbed on board. As she inched her way toward the back, 'Tricia Ann noticed that there were no seats left behind the Jim Crow sign. So she stood up and gave Mrs. Grannell hers.

"It's not fair," she said, glaring at the empty seats up front.

"No, but that's the way it is, honey," said Mrs. Grannell.

"I don' understand why—" she began. But by now the bus had reached 'Tricia Ann's stop in front of Capitol Square in the heart of downtown. The doors swung open and she hurried off.

"Carry yo'self proud," Mrs. Grannell called out the window as the bus pulled away.

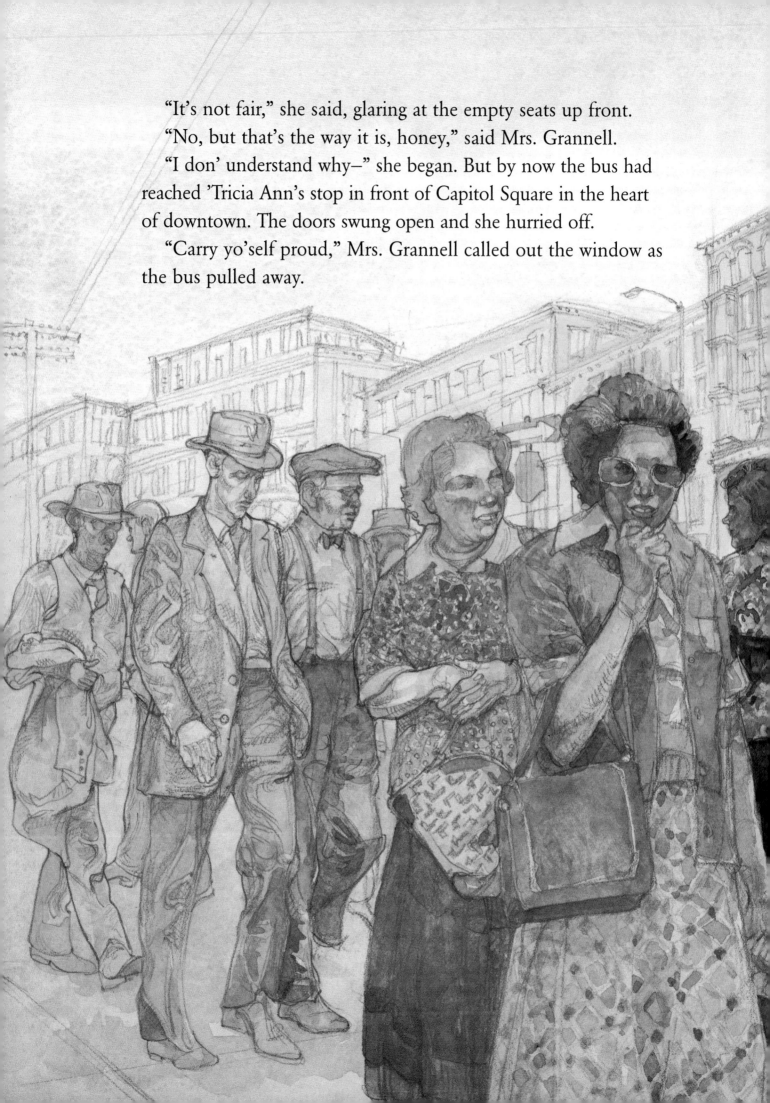

Holding her hat, 'Tricia Ann leaned back as far as she could to see Peace Fountain's magnificent water show. It made her dizzy to watch the sprays that shot high into the air, but she liked the feeling and turned 'round and 'round with her arms outstretched. Then, giggling, she staggered on wobbly legs to a nearby bench.

Instantly, 'Tricia Ann leaped to her feet.
On the bench was a sign that said: FOR WHITES ONLY.
Her face fell, and she wished for Mama Frances's
strong hand to hold. "Silly signs," she muttered as she
strutted away on sober legs.

At the edge of the square, she greeted Jimmy Lee, a street vendor. "What's got yo' face all clouded up like a stormy day?" he asked, handing 'Tricia Ann a free pretzel.

"Jim Crow makes me so mad!" she said. "My grandfather was a stonemason on Peace Fountain. Why can't I sit down and enjoy it?"

Jimmy Lee pointed to a sign in Monroe's Restaurant window. He said, "My brother cooks all the food they serve, but do you think we can sit at one of their tables and have a BLT and a cup of coffee together?" Then with a chuckle he whispered, "Not that I'd want to eat anything Jesse cooks. That man can't even now scald water."

The light changed and 'Tricia Ann carefully started across the street. "Don't let those signs steal yo' happiness," Jimmy Lee called after her.

'Tricia Ann pulled her shoulders back and fixed her thoughts on being inside that warm and welcoming place where there were no signs. Hurrying up Tenth Avenue, she passed the filling station, and stopped to buy a pop to wash down Jimmy Lee's pretzel.

At the second light, the Southland Hotel rose up in front of her, as spectacular as a palace. Mr. John Willis, the hotel's doorman, saw her. "I b'lieve an angel done slipped 'way from heaven," he said, smiling.

'Tricia Ann managed to smile back. Mr. John Willis always said the nicest things. "No, sir. It's just me."

"Your mouth is smiling, but your eyes aren't," he said.

Just then a long white car with two police escorts pulled up in front of the hotel. A man with black shiny hair and shy eyes stepped out. Suddenly people were everywhere, screaming and begging for his autograph. 'Tricia Ann got caught in the crowd and swept inside.

So often she'd wondered what it would feel like to walk on the royal red carpet that covered the double-winding staircase, or to stand in the light of the chandelier that looked like a million diamonds strung together. Now, there she was—smack in the middle of the Southland Hotel's grand lobby.

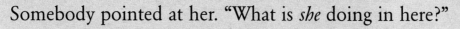

Somebody pointed at her. "What is *she* doing in here?"

It seemed as if the whole world had stopped talking, stopped moving, and was staring at her. The manager pushed his way to the front of the crowd. "What makes you think you can come inside? No colored people are allowed!" And he shooed the girl away with his arms.

'Tricia Ann backed out, shaking her head. "I-I didn't mean . . . ," she said, trying hard not to cry.

Hurrying past Mr. John Willis, 'Tricia Ann ran straight into the Mission Church ruins where Mama Frances often stopped to rest. There in the protection of the walled garden, the girl let the tears come. "Getting to Someplace Special isn't worth it," she sobbed. "I'm going home."

"My flowers have been watered already," came a voice above her. It was Blooming Mary, an elderly woman who took care of the garden with neither permission nor pay. Everybody said she was addled, but Mama Frances didn't agree. "Blooming Mary is a kind and gentle soul," she'd told 'Tricia Ann.

"You lost, child?" the woman asked.

Trying to steady her voice, 'Tricia Ann answered. "No, ma'am, I just wish my grandmother was here to help me get to Someplace Special."

"You can't get there by yourself?"

"It's too hard. I need my grandmother."

Blooming Mary nodded and thought on the matter.

Then she said, "I believe your granny *is* here, just as my granny is here with me even as I speak.
Listen close. Tell me what you hear."

All 'Tricia Ann heard was the distant buzz of a bumblebee. What was Blooming Mary talking about?

But as she listened closer, she began to hear her grandmother's steady voice. "You are somebody, a human being—no better, no worse than anybody else in this world. Gettin' someplace special is not an easy route. But don't study on quittin', just keep walking straight ahead—and you'll make it."

'Tricia Ann recalled these words from many conversations they'd had in this quiet place. They were so comforting, she didn't feel alone anymore. She wiped her eyes and straightened her hat. "You were right, ma'am," the girl told Blooming Mary. "Mama Frances is here. And she wouldn't want me to turn back."

"So, you aren't lost after all," said Blooming Mary, giving 'Tricia Ann a bright orange zinnia.

"No, ma'm, I'm not." And saying good-bye, she headed, real determined–like, on her way.

Two blocks later 'Tricia Ann came to the Grand Music Palace, where a group had gathered for the matinee performance. As the girl approached, a little boy spoke to her. "Howdy, I'm Hickey and I'm six years old today. You comin' in?"

Before 'Tricia Ann could answer, an older girl grabbed his hand. "Hush, boy," she said through clenched teeth. "Colored people can't come in the front door. They got to go 'round back and sit up in the Buzzard's Roost. Don't you know nothing?" his sister whispered harshly.

Hickey looked at 'Tricia Ann with wide, wondering eyes. "Are you going to sit up there?"

"In the last three rows of the balcony? Why, I wouldn't sit up there even if watermelons bloomed in January. Besides, I'm going to someplace very, very special," she answered, and then 'Tricia Ann skipped away.

"I want to go where she's goin'," she heard Hickey say as his sister pulled him through the door.

At the corner 'Tricia Ann saw a building rising above all that
surrounded it, looking proud in the summer sun. It was much more
than bricks and stone. It was an idea. Mama Frances called it a doorway
to freedom. When she looked at it, she didn't feel angry or hurt or
embarrassed. "At last," she whispered, "I've made it to Someplace Special."

Before bounding up the steps and through the front door, 'Tricia Ann stopped to look up at the message chiseled in stone across the front facing: PUBLIC LIBRARY: ALL ARE WELCOME.

Author's Note

This is my story. Although the setting has been fictionalized, the events are taken from my own childhood growing up in Nashville, Tennessee.

Nashville, like most southern cities in the 1950s, was segregated. The doors of hotels, restaurants, churches, and amusement parks were posted with Jim Crow segregation signs that barred African Americans, who also had to endure the further indignities of riding in the backs of buses, attending separate schools, sitting in the last rows of the balcony, and drinking from separate water fountains. But, in the late 1950s, Nashville's public library board of directors quietly voted to integrate all their facilities. The downtown branch was one of the few places where there were no Jim Crow signs and blacks were treated with some respect.

Most African American parents waited until their children were mature enough to cope with segregation before allowing them to venture outside their communities alone. I was almost twelve when my parents trusted me to make the trek to the library by myself. But like 'Tricia Ann, I had been fortified with enough love, respect, and pride to overcome any situation I encountered. Along the way, I had to face all kinds of racial bigotry and discrimination. But, for me, the library was always filled with a specialness that made the effort worthwhile. Since I felt welcome there, I checked out books more often. And the more I read, the better I understood why my grandmother believed the library was someplace more exciting, more interesting, and more informative than hotels, movies, restaurants, and amusement parks. She, like Andrew Carnegie, whose great wealth helped to build the library, knew that "reading is the doorway to freedom."

Patricia C. McKissack
Chesterfield, Missouri

PUBLIC LIBRARY: ALL ARE WELCOME.